TUNES vs. GOONS

A Random House PICTUREBACK® Book

Random House New York

Copyright © 2021 Warner Bros. Entertainment Inc.
SPACE JAM: A NEW LEGACY and all related characters
and elements © & ™ Warner Bros. Entertainment Inc.
WB SHIELD: ™ & © WBEI. (s21)

Published in the United States by Random House Children's Books, a division of Penguin Random House LLC, 1745 Broadway, New York, NY 10019, and in Canada by Penguin Random House Canada Limited, Toronto. Pictureback, Random House, and the Random House colophon are registered trademarks of Penguin Random House LLC.
rhcbooks.com
ISBN 978-0-593-38236-3 (trade) – ISBN 978-0-593-38237-0 (ebook)
Printed in the United States of America
10 9 8 7 6 5 4 3 2 1

LeBron James

One of the most talented athletes of the twenty-first century, LeBron James, aka King James, is known for his passion on and off the court. A dedicated father, LeBron will do anything—even become animated to travel through the different Warner Bros. worlds—to rescue his son. LeBron's head is in the game, and he is ready to get the Tune Squad into shape!

+ + + + PLAYER STATS + + + +

TEAM:	The Tune Squad
POSITION:	Power Forward
BRINGS TO THE TEAM:	Expertise, skill, and determination
HOMETOWN:	Akron, OH

Bugs Bunny

A smart and mischievous bunny, Bugs is used to being in the spotlight and feels lost when all his friends leave for newer franchises. He's happy to see LeBron when he lands in Looney Tunes World, and leads the charge to travel the Serververse and put together the Tune Squad. Once the team is assembled, Bugs likes to keep things fun and light, which really comes in handy during the big game!

+ + + + PLAYER STATS + + + +	
TEAM:	The Tune Squad
POSITION:	Power Forward
BRINGS TO THE TEAM:	Looney, fun, unique attitude
SPECIAL MOVE:	Hoppin' Hook Shot

Lola Bunny

A star basketball player, Lola has stellar moves on the court that are sure to give the Tunes a leg up against the Goon Squad. Tough and no-nonsense, Lola and LeBron get along well because they have the same point of view on how to win the game—with hard work and lots of practice.

+ + + + PLAYER STATS + + + +

TEAM:	The Tune Squad
POSITION:	Small Forward
BRINGS TO THE TEAM:	Talent and determination
SPECIAL MOVE:	Lola Layup

Daffy Duck

This wacky duck can be pretty bossy, which makes him the perfect coach for the Tune Squad! He commits 110 percent to everything he does, from his hero career in Metropolis to cheering on the Tune Squad from the sidelines—especially if it helps sell team merch!

+ + + + PLAYER STATS + + + +

TEAM:	The Tune Squad
POSITION:	Coach
BRINGS TO THE TEAM:	Motivational skills
SPECIAL MOVE:	Daffy's Defensive Strategy

Elmer Fudd

All that running to chase a silly rabbit puts Elmer in great shape for some cross-court sprints. He's a tireless competitor who will never give up!

+ + + + PLAYER STATS + + + +	
TEAM:	The Tune Squad
POSITION:	Shooting Guard
BRINGS TO THE TEAM:	Focus and strength
SPECIAL MOVE:	Fudd Free Frow

Foghorn Leghorn

Strong and confident, Foghorn Leghorn is the perfect defensive player! This big rooster has an even bigger voice, so the opposing team can always hear Foghorn coming.

+ + + + PLAYER STATS + + + +

TEAM:	The Tune Squad
POSITION:	Center
BRINGS TO THE TEAM:	Size and strength
QUOTE:	"I say, I say—that foul was lower than a snake full o' buckshot!"

Gossamer

Known for his hair-raising high-post moves, Gossamer could give any opponent a fright! This orange, furry creature can usually be found at center court. He's very light on his feet for such a big fella, thanks to his killer kicks!

＋＋＋＋ PLAYER STATS ＋＋＋＋

TEAM:	The Tune Squad
POSITION:	Center
BRINGS TO THE TEAM:	Size and intimidation factor
FOR THE GAG REEL:	Gossamer sometimes deflates the ball with his long nails!

Granny

× × × × × × × × × × × × ×

She may look like a sweet, harmless grandma, but Granny has some tricks up her sleeve! As the oldest member of the Tune Squad, she brings patience and knowledge that some of the more enthusiastic team members are lacking.

+ + + + PLAYER STATS + + + +

TEAM:	The Tune Squad
POSITION:	Shooting Guard
BRINGS TO THE TEAM:	Veteran leadership and patience
QUOTE:	"I got this whippersnapper."

Marvin the Martian

Marvin is on the team because Bugs took his ship to gather the others . . . but he really loves the team jersey!

+ + + + PLAYER STATS + + + +

TEAM:	The Tune Squad
POSITION:	Transportation
BRINGS TO THE TEAM:	A spaceship
QUOTE:	"I am very angry!"

Penelope Pussycat

She may be shy, but when Penelope sets her mind to something, she goes all out! Light on her feet, this fearless feline can move around the court without the other team knowing she's coming!

+ + + + PLAYER STATS + + + +

TEAM:	The Tune Squad
POSITION:	Point Guard
BRINGS TO THE TEAM:	Passion
SPECIAL MOVE:	Fast furry feet

Porky Pig

XXXXXXXXXXXXXX

Porky's nervousness makes people underestimate him, but with a little support, he can accomplish anything!

++++ PLAYER STATS ++++	
TEAM:	The Tune Squad
POSITION:	Small Forward
BRINGS TO THE TEAM:	Awesome rap skills
NEW CATCHPHRASE:	"That's *ball*, folks!"

Yosemite Sam

This short cowboy has an even shorter temper, so anyone looking to get in his way on the court had better watch out! That includes the refs, who Sam is known to argue with: "Call a foul already, ya darn galoots!"

+ + + + PLAYER STATS + + + +

TEAM:	The Tune Squad
POSITION:	Center
BRINGS TO THE TEAM:	Rootin', tootin' fighting spirit
SPECIAL MOVE:	Yosemite Slam

Road Runner

The quick and cunning Road Runner is a player the other team will never see coming!

+ + + + **PLAYER STATS** + + + +	
TEAM:	The Tune Squad
POSITION:	Point Guard
BRINGS TO THE TEAM:	Speed and craftiness
QUOTE:	"BEEP! BEEP!"

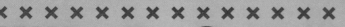

Wile E. Coyote

A master at making elaborate plans that fall apart, only to try again, Wile E. is sure to motivate the Tune Squad! He's never far from an Acme box, making him the go-to coyote for special tips and tricks.

+ + + + PLAYER STATS + + + +

TEAM:	The Tune Squad
POSITION:	Power Forward
BRINGS TO THE TEAM:	Always thinking outside the (Acme) box
SPECIAL MOVE:	Wile E.'s Acme Multiplying Machine Box

Speedy

His small size and tremendous speed make getting around the court a breeze for Speedy! But he may not be the best player to put by the net—he's not quite tall enough to make a shot.

++++ PLAYER STATS ++++

TEAM:	The Tune Squad
POSITION:	Point Guard
BRINGS TO THE TEAM:	Speed
SPECIAL MOVE:	Speedy Swish

Taz

Taz is a true wild card—no one knows what he'll do! The refs have a hard time keeping track of him because of his aggressive spinning on the court, which can help or hurt the Tunes, depending on which basket he's whirling toward.

+ + + + PLAYER STATS + + + +

TEAM:	The Tune Squad
POSITION:	Point Guard
BRINGS TO THE TEAM:	Unpredictability
SPECIAL MOVE:	Taz Tornado

Sylvester

While he's not the fastest Tune on the team, Sylvester never gives up on a chase, whether it's for Tweety or a basketball!

+ + + + PLAYER STATS + + + +

TEAM:	The Tune Squad
POSITION:	Shooting Guard
BRINGS TO THE TEAM:	Persistence
SPECIAL MOVE:	Sylvester's Switch-Up

Tweety

Don't be fooled by his sweet looks and tiny size—Tweety is an aggressive player with his eyes on the prize!

+ + + + PLAYER STATS + + + +	
TEAM:	The Tune Squad
POSITION:	Power Forward
BRINGS TO THE TEAM:	Quick on his feet and with his wings
SPECIAL MOVE:	Tweety Three-Pointer

Dom James

Dom, LeBron's son, is captain of the Goon Squad, and he developed the digital video game basketball match they're all going to compete in. Al G. has convinced Dom that the only way to earn his dad's respect is to beat him at a basketball game of his own making, but Dom is impressed when his dad shows up to the game with the Tune Squad. Will Dom stay with the Goons or decide to join the Tunes?

The Goon Squad

Using stats from real basketball players and upgrading them with amazing special skills, Al G. and Dom created an elite basketball team that is not at all what LeBron and the Tune Squad are expecting. Check out the star players!

The Brow

Arachnneka

Al G. Rhythm

The self-proclaimed king of the Serververse, Al G. Rhythm is sick of staying out of the spotlight. So he has cooked up a foolproof plot to kidnap one of the most followed people on social media—LeBron James—and use his huge platform for himself! The final step of Al G.'s master plan is to beat LeBron at his own game: basketball! With his trusty sidekick, Pete, Al G. has the upper hand on the court and in the Serververse . . . but do he and his team of Goons have what it takes to defeat the Tune Squad?